JESSIXA BAGLEY

Henry and Bea

NEAL PORTER BOOKS

HOLIDAY HOUSE/NEW YORK

For everyone, because everyone needs a friend to talk to.

Neal Porter Books

Text and illustrations copyright © 2019 by Jessixa Bagley
All Rights Reserved
HOLIDAY HOUSE is registered in the U.S. Patent and Trademark Office.
Printed and bound in June 2019 at Tien Wah Press, Johor Bahru, Johor, Malaysia.
The artwork for this book was created with watercolor and pencil on paper.
Book design by Jennifer Browne
www.holidayhouse.com
First Edition
1   3   5   7   9   10   8   6   4   2

Library of Congress Cataloging-in-Publication Data

Names: Bagley, Jessixa, author, illustrator.
Title: Henry and Bea / Jessixa Bagley.
Description: First edition. | New York : Holiday House, [2019] | "Neal Porter
Books." | Summary: When Bea's best friend, Henry, seems sad and stops
talking to her, she gently tries to find out what is wrong.
Identifiers: LCCN 2018042405 | ISBN 9780823442843 (hardcover)
Subjects: | CYAC: Best friends—Fiction. | Friendship—Fiction. | Loss
(Psychology)—Fiction. | School field trips—Fiction.
Classification: LCC PZ7.1.B3 Hen 2019 | DDC [E]—dc23 LC record available at
https://lccn.loc.gov/2018042405

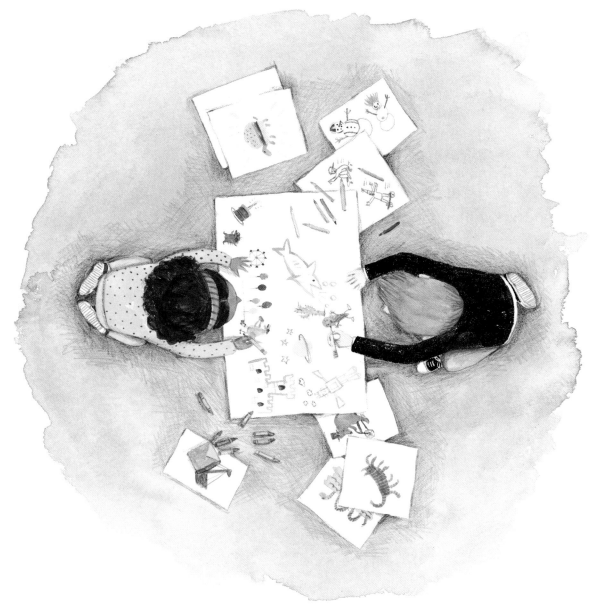

It's always lucky to find someone who understands you,
and that's why Henry and Bea were the best of friends.

They always had
fun together.

It's as if they could tell what
the other was thinking
without saying a word.

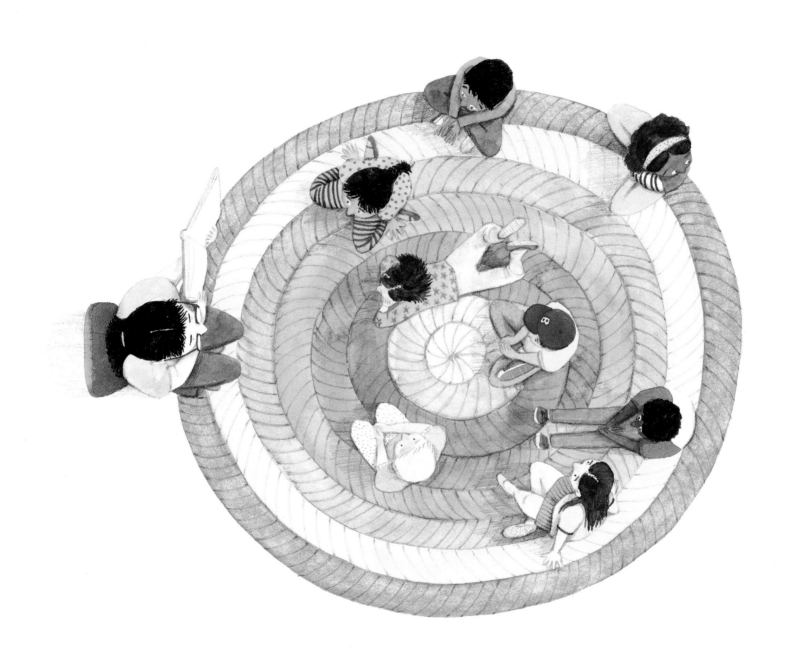

Except for one day, when Henry seemed quiet and sad.

No one, not even Bea, knew why.

"I want to sit by myself," said Henry at lunchtime.

She tried to find out what was the matter,
but Henry acted like they weren't even friends.

"What did I do?" asked Bea.

"Just leave me alone," said Henry.

And she did.

It was hard on Bea. She missed her friend.

Then Mrs. Birchfield made an announcement.
"This Friday we are taking a field trip to my family's farm!"
The classroom buzzed with excitement.
Except for Henry.

"This is going to be great!" Bea turned
and said to Henry out of habit.

"Hmph," mumbled Henry.

The morning of the field trip was cold and gray.
The class gathered outside to get onto the bus.

Neither Henry nor Bea had been to a farm, and Bea thought maybe the field trip might make him feel happier.

"Can I sit by you?" Bea gently asked Henry.

"I don't care," he huffed, and he looked the other way.

CHEWBiES

The bus rumbled up to the old farm and rolled past the
brightly colored autumn trees as the cows chewed
on the dewy morning grass.

The class was given a tour
of how the farm was run.

But Henry was still having a tough time
and went off on his own again.

When Bea opened the barn door, the air was musty and dark with old tools and tractors quietly rusting away. Her warm breath cut through the darkness.

She spied Henry in the hayloft, and climbed up,
a little reluctantly.

"I found this," said Henry without looking at Bea.

It was an old cat collar. The leather strap was
tattered and broken, and the dirt from age
made the tag hard to read.

Henry started to cry.

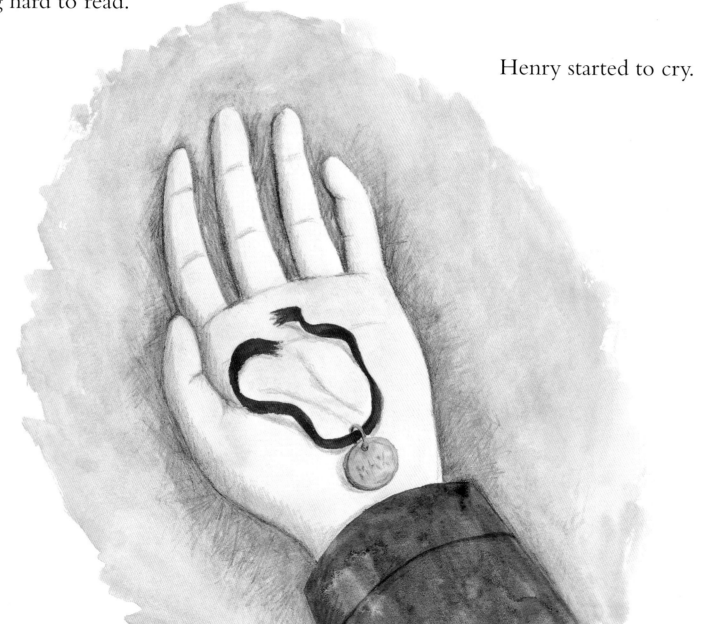

Bea froze. "What's wrong?"

"Buddy died last week," said Henry, wiping his eyes.

"Oh," said Bea. "I didn't know. He was such a sweet old cat."

"It's hard to lose a friend," she said quietly.

Bea gently put the collar back into Henry's hand.

Just then a loud rumble in the distance cut through the air. The barn door creaked open loudly.

"Bea? Henry?" called Mrs. Birchfield.

"We're up here!" Bea responded quickly.

Henry rushed to wipe his face.

"Everyone needs to come inside.
A storm is coming."

Bea and Henry climbed down from the hayloft in silence.
Then, as they were walking back to the farmhouse,
Bea got an idea.

"Wait!" she said to Henry, and grabbed a small
  shovel that was resting on a bench. She
  began to dig a hole next to the barn.
"Let's say good-bye to Buddy."

Henry nodded as he wiped away
  a few remaining tears.

Henry placed the collar in the hole and together they covered it carefully. They heard the soft sprinkle of rain hit the dirt.

The dark clouds came up behind them and filled the
sky. The rain started to come down even harder.
The rest of the class squealed with excitement
as they ran into the farmhouse.

Henry and Bea were the last to make it there.
But Henry stopped at the steps.

Bea understood.
"I won't say anything," she said quietly.

As the class got out of their muddy boots and ate some freshly baked cookies, they all chattered about the things they had seen.

Henry looked out the window.

"Maybe we'll see some lightning!" he mumbled
   to Bea through a mouthful of cookie.

"Yeah," said Bea, chomping down on one of her own.

"Or maybe even a rainbow."